PUFFIN BOOKS

THE BUNCH FROM BANANAS

The steamy coastal town of Santa Margarita del Banana is notable for two things: for its bananas, which are world-famous because they curve the other way, and for Bernard the Boy Detective.

Bernard's career starts with his brilliant and ingenious ambush of Diablo Dick – who is admittedly the most unsuccessful bandit in history. He solves the most baffling cases, including the theft of Sir George Mindbright Wilderness's entire house, and even manages to foil the High-tailed Red Banana-bending Crows.

The people in Santa Margarita del Banana are a pretty weird bunch: not just Bernard and Diablo Dick, but also ex-sleuth Big Fat Joe, the stupidest boy in school, Little Jim Winze, the town barber Hairy von Rijn, and many others. But at least there's plenty to laugh at when the bunch from Bananas are around.

For 9- to 11-year-olds.

DAVID POWNALL

The Bunch from Bananas

ILLUSTRATED BY

FREIRE WRIGHT

PUFFIN BOOKS

Puffin Books, Penguin Books Ltd, Harmondsworth, Middlesex, England
Penguin Books, 625 Madison Avenue, New York, New York 10022, U.S.A.
Penguin Books Australia Ltd, Ringwood, Victoria, Australia
Penguin Books Canada Ltd, 2801 John Street, Markham, Ontario, Canada L3R 1B4
Penguin Books (N.Z.) Ltd, 182-190 Wairau Road, Auckland 10, New Zealand

—

First published by Victor Gollancz Ltd, 1980
Published in Puffin Books 1982

—

Copyright © David Pownall, 1980
Illustrations copyright © Freire Wright, 1980
All rights reserved

—

Reproduced, printed and bound in Great Britain by
Cox & Wyman Ltd., Reading

For Dale who is forty
Gareth who is fourteen
Tom who is four

Contents

CHAPTER ONE

The Use of Cover

The small town of Santa Margarita del Banana stands on a desert coastline near some mountains. It is so far from other places that no one bothers to think about what country it is in. Some Indians who live in comfortable caves nearby say that the town was started by men from the stars who came down for a visit thousands of years ago. Other people think that this idea is far-fetched.

The fields around the town are green and well-watered. The farmers grow many different kinds of vegetables and fruit. The most popular crop is bananas. The bananas of Santa Margarita del Banana are world-famous because they curve the other way.

The town is a happy place for most days of the week. It has a great cathedral which has three red towers, and a bishop. It has a supermarket called O.K. Bazaars run by Bertha Boom-Boom who is the girl-friend of Big Fat Joe the retired detective who needs no description. Other characters in the town can be seen in the street or sitting in Lugsy's cantina in

the evening having a cool drink. They seem to be enjoying life and often smile.

Hairy von Rjin smiles a lot but it cannot be seen. He has never had his hair cut in his life, and he is the town barber. When he stands in his shop doorway all his face is hidden by black curly hair except for his eyes and nose. Hairy von Rjin hates all forms of advertising.

His shop is next to the cathedral. It overlooks the statue to Ug the Indescribable, the inventor of electricity, which dominates the square. In the summer, butterflies alight on Hairy von Rjin's beard and on his head and make him look as though he is wearing jewellery. When his long curly black beard falls down the steps into the gutter during the rainy season, mice and ants hold on to it to stop themselves from drowning.

Today the barber is leaning against the door-post playing with his silver scissors. They flash in the sun and the snip-snip can be heard over the square like a bird song.

This morning the retired detective, Big Fat Joe, has brought his son Bernard along for a hair-cut. The boy can be cheeky when he is in the mood.

As Hairy von Rjin put the wooden plank across the arms of the barber's chair for Bernard to sit on, Bernard grabbed his beard and swung himself up into position.

"Bernard! Behave yourself!" Big Fat Joe shouted, red in the face with embarrassment. "How dare you take such liberties!"

"No matter," Hairy von Rjin grumbled casually, "just as long as he cuts out that kind of trick before he weighs as much as you."

Big Fat Joe sighed and left the shop. Once again he was having to suffer for Bernard's low standard of conduct. What was he going to do with the boy to keep him out of mischief? As he crossed the square towards O.K. Bazaars and some black coffee and jam scones with his girl-friend, the ex-detective was worried.

"He showed me up in front of Hairy," Big Fat Joe complained a few minutes later as he sat with Bertha Boom-Boom in her sitting-room which was furnished with crates and boxes from the supermarket, "he made me feel ashamed."

"He needs a hobby," Bertha Boom-Boom advised. "His mind is too active. Give him something to do."

"What?" asked Big Fat Joe as he quietly admired Bertha Boom-Boom's latest hair-style which was shaped like a tea-cosy full of house-bricks. "I can't think of anything."

As Big Fat Joe chatted to his beautiful girl-friend from the depths of a cardboard box which had *Spanish Firelighters* written across it in stencilled letters, a bandit was creeping through the back door of Hairy von Rjin's shop. In his right hand was a big rusty revolver.

"Grab the clouds!" he ordered fiercely.

"Diablo Dick!" Hairy von Rjin gasped. "I thought you were in the jug."

Diablo Dick laughed. He boasted to the barber about how he had escaped from the prison by keeping all the spaghetti served to him until it went stale, then tying it all together and making a long pole with which he had vaulted over the wall. While he was bragging he did not notice Bernard hiding himself in Hairy von Rjin's beard.

"Now open the till!" Diablo Dick demanded in a drawl.

Hairy von Rjin shuffled across the shop and put his key in the till. He went quite slowly because he had Bernard hanging on to his beard, completely covered up. When the till was unlocked the drawer shot out with the clang of a bell. When Diablo Dick saw all the money he rushed forward and started to fill his pockets. Bernard waited for exactly the right moment, then, swinging forward, he kicked the rusty revolver out of the bandit's hand and slammed the till

drawer shut on the other one. As the revolver hit the ground it went off and blew a hole in a vat of perfumed hair oil which poured down Diablo Dick's face so he could not see. Hairy von Rjin knelt down and swiftly tied the bandit's ankles together with his own long moustache. The knot he used is called a clove hitch.

"Run and fetch the sheriff!" the barber mumbled as the writhing, cursing, struggling bandit dragged him all over the floor. "I'll keep this fellow hobbled here."

Bernard had no need to run for help as a crowd of townspeople arrived carrying the drooping figure of Dormitory McBride, the town sheriff, who had been having his mid-morning siesta. When he had been awakened and told of the shot heard at Hairy von Rjin's, Dormitory had sniffed the air for gunsmoke but had only caught the wonderful niff of the hair oil. This had reminded him of the dream he had just been having in which he was sleeping in a hammock in a rose-garden dreaming another dream . . . so Dormitory had turned over and gone back to sleep. When he opened his eyes and recognised the bandit who was now hauling Hairy von Rjin out of his own front door by the moustache, Dormitory immediately exclaimed:

"Well, I'm danged, hornswoggled and panhandled, if it ain't Diablo Dick from the mountains. There's a reward out for him . . . zzzzzzzzzzz," and went back to sleep in a great heap of hair-cuttings.

At that moment Big Fat Joe came puffing into the shop still stuck in the box of Spanish Firelighters. He had heard the shot and run across as soon as he could. Recognising Diablo Dick as an old adversary who had often escaped from his clutches by his wiles and illicit skills, Big Fat Joe hauled the raging bandit to his feet, untied Hairy von Rjin's moustache, then snapped a pair of handcuffs on to Diablo Dick's wrists.

"So, we meet again," he wheezed. "Got you this time."

"No you didn't! Don't you go trying to take all the glory!" Diablo Dick snorted. "It was this kid here who captured me, not you, you old buffalo-brained boiler!"

Bernard looked up into his father's face. As he told the full story of his brilliant and ingenious ambush of Diablo Dick from the depths of Hairy von Rjin's beard, Bernard anxiously watched Big Fat Joe's eyes for signs of approval. There was a struggle going on, yes, a hint of envy, and here a left-over of the humiliation of being called a buffalo-brained boiler, but the blue eyes of the ex-detective soon blazed with one emotion—sheer gladness. He had had an idea.

"Why don't you take up this kind of a thing as a hobby," he said to Bernard as Diablo Dick was led away to the sheriff's office where buckets of cold water were being thrown over Dormitory McBride to wake him up, and buckets of hot water prepared for Diablo Dick to wash the smell of the hair oil off him as it was attracting the Four-nosed Stinkwort Scorpion-eating June Bugs from the mountain slopes in swarms.

So ambition was born in Bernard, and a hobby

found for him. From that day on he knew that his future life was mapped out for him.

Hairy von Rjin became more cautious and keeps his back door locked now. Also he keeps his till hanging on a chain under his beard which makes him stoop so he looks older than he actually is. Whenever bandits come into his shop for a hair-cut or to rob him, Hairy pleads poverty and offers to make up for it by giving them a short back and sides for nix. The bandits usually go away satisfied. If they get mad, as one or two have, and try to belt the barber then they bash their knuckles on the till and run out crying.

This is a good crime prevention system for barbers who have never had their hair cut but it is lousy business and you won't see it advertised anywhere.

Diablo Dick got five years and a week for attempted armed robbery and he was locked away in a prison where there is no spaghetti on the menu, though they do sometimes serve apple dumplings.

We will meet him again, no doubt.

CHAPTER TWO

A Hard Case

Bernard had an interest in lizards. He often used to walk out into the desert and look under stones, noting the different types and colours as the little reptiles scuttled away and how their strange eyes were like ball–bearings swivelling in their flat heads.

One day Bernard was out in the desert when he was caught in a cloudburst. The rain came down so heavily that he could not see his hand in front of his face. When it stopped and the sun came out again, the desert steamed. Bernard wrung his clothes out and put them on a rock to dry. Then he looked under the rock for lizards.

The rain had made a big puddle of mud and dirt under the rock and there was something moving in it.

"Well, how amazing!" Bernard breathed. "They can even turn a deep shade of brown."

"Who can?" came a voice out of the puddle.

"Why, you can lizard," Bernard replied, delighted to find one that could talk.

"Who are you calling lizard?" demanded a small man, levering himself up on one elbow. "My name is

Senor Gonzalez Filth and I am bivouacing here for my summer holidays."

Bernard retreated a step or two as the mucky little fellow rolled from under the rock and flexed his grimy muscles.

"Well? Want a fight?" he shouted.

"No, not at all," Bernard replied, retreating. "Don't hit me, please."

"Why, you're only a lad, a mere child." The grubby little fellow beamed a mud-cracking smile. "Would you like to learn a few ruses from a troglodyte?"

Bernard accepted gladly and put his clothes back on, then followed Senor Gonzalez Filth along a trail which led through the mountains towards Santa Margarita del Banana. From the top of the pass they could see the sapphire ocean and all down the coast.

When they got near to the road Bernard asked Senor Gonzalez Filth if he could start learning something quite soon as it was nearly time for his tea. They could make a good beginning by discussing what a troglodyte was.

"Someone who lives in a hole. Take me, for instance. In the city where I work as a dustman, I live in a dustbin, an inside-out hole if you like. On holiday ... well, what a man needs is a home from home. Yes, we'll have that fellow's sandwiches."

A group of workmen were erecting a triumphal arch over the road which led from the mountains to the town. They were all up ladders with wire, flowers and buckets of paint. The arch was to welcome visitors who would be coming to the Fiesta of Ug the Indescribable which started on Saturday.

Under Bernard's astonished eyes, Senor Gonzalez Filth crept behind a bush and hooked a bucket of yellow paint with a thorn twig, opened it, then poured the contents over himself. Then he strolled across the desert sand to the workmen's van, put his hand through the window and took the largest lunch-packet that was on the seat.

The men up the ladders did not see him at all. To them he was invisible.

"Camouflage!" Senor Gonzalez Filth giggled as he undid the sandwiches, putting yellow fingerprints all over the bread. Bernard could not bring himself to accept any of the food. He was deeply upset.

"That's stealing!" he hissed.

"I'm starving!" Senor Gonzalez Filth hissed back,

his eyes flashing. "What are you going to do? Report me?"

"That doesn't make it right!" Bernard almost shouted.

"No, but it makes it practical!" the sticky, yellow troglodyte replied, biting into another sandwich. "Go away. You're a nuisance, and, what is worse, you don't understand."

Bernard retreated through the cactus plants and thorn bushes until he was well clear of the road, then sat down and had a long think. There was only one person he could ask for advice; his father, Big Fat Joe.

When Bernard arrived home Big Fat Joe was polishing his magnifying-glass with a soft yellow duster and looking at his own fingers through it.

"There's not much to be said about fingers," he was muttering, "but a lot about finger-prints. I thought my nails were clean but . . . look at that. Dirt. I couldn't see it, but it was there."

This was a good train of thought for a man in Big Fat Joe's position as he had retired from active life and could spend time looking for small but interesting details. Last week he had been giving much consideration to atom bombs and atoms, mighty universes and molecules and humming-birds.

At the end of Bernard's tale about Senor Gonzalez Filth the ex-detective spent a few moments explaining his views on theft—which were very simple—then he frog-marched Bernard round to the garage, pushed him into his orange drop-head Bugatti and drove like the wind to the place where the workmen were erecting the triumphal arch. When they arrived there was a crowd gathered round a thorn-bush and a strange croaking sound coming from the centre of it. Big Fat Joe jostled his way through the workmen, Bernard on his heels, and they looked down.

Senor Gonzalez Filth was lying on his back, a sandwich jammed between his teeth, his arms and legs sticking straight out, his hair standing on end, a brilliant glossy yellow all over. The paint had dried and left him like that. Only his eyes could move and they slid from side to side, two brown, pleading mice in a cage of rigid eyelashes.

"You see son," Big Fat Joe said with measured satisfaction. "Even Nature is against stealing. Who did this? The sun. Does that answer your question?"

It didn't, Bernard thought, but what did it matter at this point? His main concern was to get Senor Gonzalez Filth back to Santa Margarita del Banana and out of the casing of paint before he died. Putting the stiff golden star of the troglodyte in the back of the Bugatti, Big Fat Joe drove back to the town and straight to the ironmonger's where he bought up all the turpentine in stock. With Bernard helping, he poured every bottle into the bath and immersed Senor Gonzalez Filth in it for six hours, then wiped him clean.

"Don't stand near the fire," Big Fat Joe warned him, "or you'll go up in a sheet of flame."

"You have saved my life. You care about me," Senor Gonzalez Filth wept. "How can I go back to the city now? You have destroyed my system. I no longer *believe* in the system. I cannot steal, yet I don't earn enough to live on honestly. I don't wish to appear ungrateful but you have, at the same time, saved my life and made it impossible for me to continue living it."

While Big Fat Joe got moody and sat in the corner trying to work this one out, Bernard ran round to the cathedral and asked to see the Bishop.

"It is a matter of life and death," he announced as the Bishop turned off his almighty television set (with the three metre screen) and gave him his undivided attention. "What can we do?"

The Bishop replied slowly, choosing his words very carefully. This was not a straightforward case and he was unused to dealing with such matters as

there was no real poverty in the town. It was outside his personal experience, but . . . .

"Yes?" Bernard cried. "Yes? Yes?"

"We should have at least one person here who *seems* to be poor, so we can remember what it is like. I will talk to the town council."

Three days later Senor Gonzalez Filth was officially appointed as The Poor of Santa Margarita del Banana. He was given a good job as the Refuse Disposal Expert, and a decent salary, but he had to promise to always look and act poor, lest the citizens forget the bottom end of the scale.

CHAPTER THREE

Following in Father's Footsteps

Bernard's best friend was Little Jim Winze who was the youngest son of the head spider-catcher on Santa Margarita del Banana's publicly-owned banana plantations. The job of head spider-catcher was passed on from father to son and Little Jim Winze was trying not to grow up because he knew that it was inevitable that he would face disappointment in mature life. As the youngest son he could never inherit his father's position, yet his greatest passion was spiders, especially the kind which live in banana plants. Little Jim Winze had refused to learn to read, write or anything about history and spent a lot of time and effort on being as backward as possible. At school he had to sit outside in the playground in a cardboard box because he was not only at the bottom of the class but beyond that. The teachers allowed him to sit out there in the sun teaching his choir of black widow spiders to sing laments rather than put up with trying to educate him.

Bernard ran out at break-time and arrived at Little Jim Winze's cardboard box just as the choir of spiders were bringing Mozart's Mass in C Minor to a close. It was the last day of term and all the children of the town had been given their examination results which had been quite good, considering. Bernard knew that this was a bad time for Little Jim Winze and he was anxious to keep his mind off the problem of being deliberately ignorant. When Little Jim Winze asked Bernard how he had done in his exams, Bernard scaled down all his marks by ten per cent which meant that he got minus three for Physics. He did this for his best friend's sake so he would not feel left out.

"What shall we do in the holidays?" Bernard asked. "Do you want to go camping like last summer?"

"No thanks," Little Jim Winze muttered, eyeing a ragged old sparrow which was trying to circle over the spiders like a hawk and constantly banging into the school flag pole. "My Dad says I'm not having

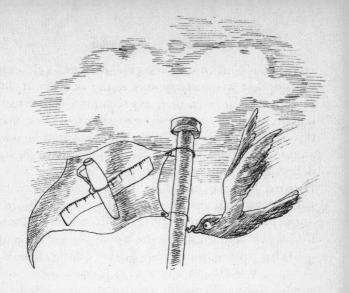

any fun at all, no playing out, no games, nothing, until I promise to try at school. He doesn't understand me."

To Bernard this was sad news. He had enough problems with his own father, Big Fat Joe, who had become jealous of Bernard's talent as a crimefighter, but here indeed was a worse case—a father who was punishing his son for wanting to be like him. What a world, Bernard thought.

"Is he going to make you sit inside all day?" he enquired, squatting down at a safe distance from the contralto section of the choir as they tuned up for a stab at "*The Red River Valley*".

"You'll lose the use of your limbs."

"He says I've nearly lost the use of my brain already, so what's the difference?"

Halting the black widow spiders in mid-phrase, his baton rapping on the asphalt with an unnecessary venom born of frustration, Little Jim Winze put them into the box and closed the lid. With the box under his arm he walked across the playground to the school gates, out into the road and headed for home on the outskirts of town, Bernard by his side.

"I honestly don't know what I'm going to do mate," Little Jim Winze sniffed. "This seems to be the crunch."

Bernard said good-bye to his friend at the edge of the banana plantation. He could see Little Jim Winze's father going through the banana plants with his net and the way that the man turned a cold eye on his son as he tramped through to the house.

"Rapscallion!" he shouted. "After all I've done for you. When I was a lad we didn't have the opportunities you have nowadays. I started work at the age of twelve. You could go to the pictures and have change out of a tanner for a three-course meal at the station buffet if you were careful . . . ."

Bernard put his hands over his ears and went home. If only there was something he could do to help his friend.

The next morning there occurred a crisis in Santa Margarita del Banana that was as regular as clockwork and considerably more dependable. Sergeant Leonard Flytrifle, a retired soldier who suffered from dark moods to do with a war which he had once fought in, climbed to the top of the cathedral tower, locked all the doors behind him, and yelled down to

the people in the square below that he felt like jumping off.

Dormitory McBride was off in the mountains looking for Diablo Dick who had escaped again. Horatio Upright was busy rescuing his mother (only for practice) from a burning paddy-field (a staple crop in the district), and could not make his services as the town hero available. Big Fat Joe no longer took Sergeant Leonard Flytrifle's threats about self-damage seriously. And the Bishop was at a conference in Mexico City.

"You'd better believe me!" the old soldier yelled, swinging one-handed from the weather-cock. "They had me marching and counter-marching for years and I can't get the bugle-calls out of my head. Even in bed I have to sleep saluting and I can't stop putting blacking on my boots even when I'm barefoot."

Lugsy came up with the suggestion that as there was a shortage of men of action in the town that day, it might be a good idea to ask Sergeant Flytrifle if there was any particular friend he would like to come and talk him down.

"I have no friends!" Sergeant Flytrifle honked as he bent back the lightning-conductor and made it vibrate like a tuning-fork. "But I might listen to any old comrade-in-arms."

The only other man who had fought in this war was Little Jim Winze's father. Hairy von Rjin pedalled off on his bicycle to the banana plantation and told him about the situation in the town square.

"He probably won't jump, but we can't take the

risk. We know that he'll be all right tomorrow, once the mood passes. Will you talk to him?"

"Old fool! He was only in the Pay Corps," Little Jim Winze's father said scornfully. "He's just trying to attract attention to himself."

"What happens if he does jump?" Hairy von Rjin insisted.

"There'll be a hole in the road," Little Jim Winze's father said curtly and, shouldering his net, marched away into the banana plants.

Hairy von Rjin was appalled. What could he do? While he was thinking about it, Little Jim Winze appeared with his cardboard box and asked Hairy von Rjin to take him into town on his cross-bar as a matter of urgency. As they sped along the bumpy cart-track of the plantation the barber kept drawing his flying beard away from the cardboard box as he could hear the black widow spiders singing, in descant "*Come Into The Garden Maud*".

When they arrived in the town square there was a cry of disgust from everyone as they heard about the callous attitude of Little Jim Winze's father. Up on the tower old Sergeant Flytrifle lodged his gleaming toe-caps in the gutter and hung upside-down like a bat in a final act of defiance against Fate.

"Even my comrades-in-arms have deserted me!" he shouted dismally.

When Little Jim Winze opened up his cardboard box everyone moved away as they knew that spiders were very poisonous. If they managed to bite someone that person would certainly die. There were also some critical remarks from people who, though they had no ideas of their own about saving the old soldier, could not see how infesting the square with singing spiders was going to help.

Bernard stuck up for his friend because he could see, vaguely, what was in Little Jim Winze's mind. With relief he recognised the headmaster of the school in the crowd. He could not deny being dazzled if this worked!

Sending the black widow spiders out in two lines, Little Jim Winze called to the left line, "Right turn," then to the right line, "Left turn," so that they formed a square. Then he produced his baton out of his pocket, hummed a note, and the spiders sang:

> *"Mellow the moonlight to shine is beginning,*
> *There in the moonlight young Eileen keeps*
> *spinning . . ."*

As they sang the old Irish song the black widows started to make a web, crossing and re-crossing the square. By the time that the spinning song was over, the web was finished but made a thousand times stronger than usual because these singing spiders were fed on spaghetti, this being Caruso's (who was the most famous singer ever known) favourite food. They were only just in time. As Lugsy grabbed hold of one corner, Bernard another, Hairy von Rjin another, and Big Fat Joe the last, Sergeant Leonard Flytrifle undid his bootlaces and slid out of his footwear, heading towards hard ground at great speed. Striking the spider's web he bounced back up again and it was five minutes before the trampoline effect subsided enough for him to step off the web and offer his thanks to Little Jim Winze who had, by that time, been recognised as a potential genius by the headmaster and taken home as his adopted son, together with the black widow spiders, which took some courage.

That night Little Jim Winze's father fell asleep in a bunch of bananas and was exported to Russia.

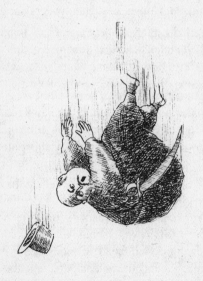

CHAPTER FOUR

Fiesta

The most famous person in the history of Santa Margarita del Banana was Ug the Indescribable who invented electricity a long time ago. No one else in the world outside the town agreed that he was the man who had done this—in fact, they insisted, no one *invented* electricity, it was just there, like Mount Everest. The citizens of Santa Margarita del Banana found this idea unacceptable and continued to immortalise their old hero (Stone Age if he was a day), and they celebrated a special fiesta in his honour each year in the third week of June. The dancing and feasting revolved around the statue of Ug the Indescribable which stood in the square. It is worth trying to describe this Indescribable fellow because he was very important.

First, he was hairy and his arms hung down past his knees. In his right hand, which was held aloft (but would have hung down past his knees had it been just hanging), was a lightning-flash to symbolise his invention. Around his waist he wore the skin of a mountain lion and on his enormous low-browed head, a hat made of a brontosaurus hoof. All this was cast in bronze and had to be polished by Senor Gonzalez Filth once a week. Getting in all the nooks and crannies of Ug the Indescribable's frowning face was a real bind to the small phenomenally grubby gaucho, Gonzalez. He did it with metal polish and an old pair of football socks.

Of all Santa Margarita del Banana's ninety-four fiestas in the year, that of Ug the Indescribable was perhaps the most popular—but not with everybody.

The Bishop did not like it. He did not like the statue being opposite the cathedral. To him, Ug the Indescribable was an insult. He was something from the olden days before the church got started. The Bishop's feelings on this subject were so strong that he had denounced the fiesta from the pulpit and demanded that a proper saint's day be put in its place. There had been many battles in the town council and bitter words had been said.

But the Bishop could not oust Ug the Indescribable from his popularity with the people. He kept his place in their hearts. Every time they turned on the light or burnt the toast, they thanked Ug.

The fiesta came round again. On the previous Sunday the Bishop became very hot under the collar during his sermon and called Ug a throwback to a pagan age, a phrase which was repeated in the local newspaper. Sir George Mindbright Wilderness, the town's rich man and magistrate, paid a visit to the Bishop and tried to get him to lay off Ug.

"He is so far in the past that he has no meaning. He

is only a connexion with ancient history," Sir George Mindbright Wilderness reasoned as he climbed into his sedan chair which was carried by four robots. "The church can't control everything back to the year dot!"

"There will be a wailing and a gnashing of teeth . . ." the Bishop started, still angry. He had already had a row with Sir George and ordered him out of the cathedral.

"Never mind all that. Why don't you go off on a holiday of your own? Leave us in peace for the fiesta?" Sir George suggested as politely as he could with the Bishop pushing him into his sedan chair. "I'll lend you my villa by the thermal spring if you like."

This made the Bishop really upset. He kicked the robot closest to him and yelled as he stubbed his toe. With a look of patient suffering on his face, Sir George Mindbright Wilderness twiddled the knobs on the control panel of the sedan chair and the robots trotted away at speed, leaving the Bishop hugging his sore toe and saying things under his breath which he had to ask forgiveness for later.

The day of the fiesta of Ug the Indescribable dawned bright and clear. All the children were up very early and out in the streets and the square in their best clothes. All the houses were hung with flags and bunting and the lightning-flash of Ug was sported in everyone's lapel on a badge which Bertha Boom-Boom had given away free with packets of ginger biscuits bought at her supermarket all that week.

The whole town was looking forward to a good time. Lugsy's cantina was crowded. There were stalls selling all kinds of hot pies and sweets and everyone who could do their stuff, did it. They did juggling and fire-eating, gymnastics and poetry-reading. By the time it came round to twelve o'clock the town was full of people and they were enjoying themselves very much. Laughter, music, smiles and embraces were everywhere that day.

Noon was the time for the traditional dancing. Wearing old battery-cases, porcelain fuses in their ear-lobes and reworked heavy-duty cable round their necks, the dancers performed the ancient steps which had been handed down from generation to generation: *Ohm Sweet Ohm*, the *Volta* and the *Watt's Cooking?* The spectators were transported back in their minds to an earlier age when things were more simple. In the final dance, the *Spark*, all the dancers leapt up and down and threw themselves in the air. This was the favourite dance with the crowd. As Hairy von Rjin hurtled through the space between Big Fat Joe and Dormitory McBride and they caught him with great skill, the crowd burst into applause. Bernard watched them perform and looked forward to the day when he would be old enough to take place in these wonderful ritual dances.

A microphone had been put on a platform. As the dances ended, Sir George Mindbright Wilderness climbed up. Cameras clicked, taking pictures of the dignified and silver-haired gentleman clearing his throat.

"Fellow citizens, once again it is my privilege to say a few words in honour of our most famous son, Ug the Indescribable, the undoubted inventor of electricity. Where would we be without it? What a blessing it is to every housewife and to our sheriff, Dormitory McBride, who can see what is happening at night by the street lamps, thereby not giving robbers a chance . . . ."

The bells in the cathedral tower began to ring.

The crowd turned their heads to see what was happening. Far above the Bishop's tiny fist appeared in the belfry, being shaken with intense ferocity.

"You see what I'm up against . . ." Sir George started to say but the bells drowned him out.

The crowd moved away after ten more minutes of bell-ringing, with disappointed faces. This was not how they had wanted to spend the fiesta. When the Bishop had finished ringing the bells, only Sir George and Bernard were left in the square, everyone else having gone home with their hands over their ears.

"Well, you've done it this time!" Sir George said into the microphone so the words boomed out over the square through the loudspeakers. "I hope you're proud of yourself."

Erect and thin the old aristocrat walked out of the square. He was having to go home by foot because the pressure of the sound from the bells had activated the sensitive brain equipment of the robots and they had run off by themselves leaving their owner stranded.

Bernard was the only person in the square when the Bishop appeared at the door of the cathedral.

"Whither has everyone fled?" he asked nervously.

"Home. They couldn't stand the din. And they're not too pleased with you wrecking the fiesta so don't look for much in the collection on Sunday," Bernard said.

"Thou art disrespectful, Bernard. I'll speak to thy father about that."

"You can speak to him but I think you'll find he won't speak to you."

"I did what I thought was right. It seemeth to have benefited me not."

So saying the Bishop turned round and went back up the cathedral steps, a sad and lonely man. When he opened the gigantic doors and slipped inside he looked like a bat entering a huge cave. The doors slammed behind him and the square was silent.

When the next fiesta for Ug the Indescribable came round, the Bishop did go to Sir George Mindbright Wilderness's villa at the thermal spring and sat in the hot water, having been in another kind of hot water for the last full year for fiesta-wrecking, something Dormitory McBride could not arrest him for but which was generally agreed to be underhand, unholy, unwholesome and unholiday-like behaviour for a bishop.

CHAPTER FIVE

A Fishy One

There were only two dogs in Santa Margarita del Banana. Whereas there were many people who kept cats, rabbits and parrots only Lugsy and Hurtle McTurtle had dogs. Lugsy kept an old spaniel with no teeth which was supposed to frighten rowdy elements out of his cantina on fiesta days and weekends when men and women got restless looking for some relaxation (it worked very well, this old spaniel, because it made everyone unbearably sad until they crept off in tears, leaving their drinks undrunk on the table); and Hurtle McTurtle had the only fishing dog in the world, an animal he had bred up from nothing which was called a Santa Magarita del Banana Piscograbber in the British Kennel Club records, or the Mad Snapper for short.

Hurtle McTurtle, dressed in his yellow oilskins which were the colour of smoked haddock, was preparing his boat for a fishing trip out into the Gulf one day when he noticed that the Mad Snapper was scenting the sea breeze and whining with excitement. This was a good sign. For the last month Hurtle

McTurtle's catches had been very small and the fish-monger was beginning to make telephone calls to fishing villages further down the coast to see if he could get supplies from elsewhere.

"Cast off Bernard!" Hurtle McTurtle called to the boy detective who had asked if he could come out on the boat for the day. "We could be on to something here!"

With a low, sweet whistle Hurtle McTurtle summoned the Mad Snapper to his side in the wheelhouse, started up the engine, and headed out to sea.

A Fishy One

The Mad Snapper went to the bow and stood as close to the edge as he could, his long thin nose thrust out over the waves, sniffing, his tail wagging with joy.

"Is he always right?" Bernard asked as the boat cleared the harbour mouth and started to bob up and down in the heavy waves.

"He has led me on a few wild goose chases, but that was in the early days while I was still training him. We once followed a petrol tanker halfway to Bolivia because it had four tons of cod in its deep freeze, but I forgave him. He's almost human, you know. All his mistakes are understandable."

"What species is it likely to be at this time of year?" Bernard enquired intelligently, having taken the trouble to do some swotting up on the seasonal migrations of fish before he came out that morning. "Could it be Nassau Groupers or Californian Sheepsheads?"

"No, I don't think so. More likely to be Amberjacks, Bonefish or Bluestriped Grunts."

"Get many Firemouth Panchax round here?" Bernard asked, hands behind his back.

"Only when they jump out of the goldfish bowl," Hurtle McTurtle smiled. "They're aquarium fish and only an inch or two long."

The boat was now about a mile out to sea and Bernard turned round to look at the town as it lay in the early morning sun under the blue haze of the mountains. He hoped that at the end of the day they would return with a lot of fish. His father, Big Fat Joe, was complaining only last night that he had had no fish to eat for a fortnight and that it was a necessary food for the brain. Even as a retired professional man he still had cause to use his mind over day-to-day items such as the laundry and the cost of cucumber seeds (one of Big Fat Joe's hobbies was the growing of giant striped cucumbers). The whole population of the town could be suffering from malnutrition of the brain right now. That faint mist over the roof-tops could be a mental fog drifting out of the ears of one and all.

The Mad Snapper reared up on his hind-legs and boxed the air with his front paws, his tail swishing like a smitten punchbag.

"Time to let the net out!" Hurtle McTurtle said, handing the wheel over to Bernard. "I think it's a good job you came along to give me a hand today. If the Mad Snapper's enthusiasm is anything to go by we should be in for a big haul."

Hurtle McTurtle paid the net over the side. Bernard kept a steady course. Suddenly the boat started going backwards and the Mad Snapper dived overboard, snarling.

"What's happening?" Bernard stammered as the stern set up a bow-wave and the flags on the mast flew in the opposite direction. "The vessel is not obeying the tiller, Captain."

But Hurtle McTurtle did not reply. He was hanging over the side and watching a submarine surface with his net wrapped round it and the Mad Snapper sinking his fangs into the conning-tower. When the hatch opened and fourteen Chinamen in naval uniforms filed out, Bernard cut the engines. The Mad Snapper immediately became friendly and allowed himself to be patted on the head while an interpreter explained that the captain of the submarine apologised to the honourable fisherman for the accident but asked if he could give a good reason why he, an alien, was fishing in Shanghai harbour? Hurtle McTurtle replied that he was only a mile or so from home, and that was a long way from Shanghai.

There was a pause as this news sank in. Then the captain asked if the honourable fisherman and his young friend were of the opinion that a Chinese submarine would be welcome in the town harbour, for

they were short of fuel and would like to buy some.

Hurtle McTurtle said that he had no doubt as to the hospitality of Santa Margarita del Banana to strangers in distress and offered to guide the submarine in once the Chinese had disentangled themselves from his net.

With the Mad Snapper standing on the conning-tower, the submarine slid into the harbour behind Hurtle McTurtle's fishing boat and was greeted by a crowd of curious citizens. Sir George Mindbright Wilderness was called for, and the Bishop, then a deal was struck with the Chinese captain. In exchange for five hundred gallons of fuel what could the captain offer?

Would the honourable citizens be prepared to accept goods? Barter? Chinese money would be of no use in the town.

"What have you got that we might like?" Sir George Mindbright Wilderness asked courteously, pouring out a cup of tea for the captain in the harbour-master's office.

"Shark-fin soup, king prawn chop suey, haddock foo yong, swordfish and bamboo-shoots, Mandarin mackerel . . . ."

On behalf of the trade delegation, Sir George Mindbright Wilderness readily accepted this offer, knowing the hunger for fish in the town. Also it was agreed that half of its value should be credited to Hurtle McTurtle who had caught the submarine.

"I'll have to breed the Mad Snapper and offer his pups on the open market," Hurtle McTurtle said wryly as he stepped out of his yellow oilskins and hung his sou'wester on the hallstand in his house. "But I think I'll change his official name to the Santa Margarita del Banana Metal–muncher."

The dog himself settled his long nose on the brass fender of the fire and fell into a well-earned sleep, dreaming of welded whales.

CHAPTER SIX

The Rivals

Horatio Upright had been the town hero for many years. He was still an active man and only last week had beaten off an attacker who threatened to fuse all Bertha Boom-Boom's supermarket trolleys together with a blow torch because she had sold him a duff tin of dog-meat. But he was very suspicious of Bernard's recent successes and complained to Big Fat Joe that the boy was trying to steal away his livelihood. Bernard was very distressed. He had never realised that he might be putting someone out of a job by helping people and saving their lives. For a month he went to school, came home, read books and watched television. He avoided any challenge or call to adventure. He became very bored. During the same period he steered clear of Horatio Upright.

"There just isn't room for both of us," he said to his reflection in the mirror as he brushed his teeth, "and he was here first."

And this was true, for Horatio Upright had five decades of heroism behind him.

Next Monday brought a disaster at the silver mine, El Dinero, which lay at the foot of the mountains to the east of Santa Margarita del Banana. The siren went in Dormitory McBride's office and he turned it off with the heel of his riding boot and went back to sleep. Sir George Mindbright Wilderness, who owned the mine, was playing darts with his butler in the games room of his vast and ornate mansion called The Bumble Bee's Nest, when the telephone rang. Calling for his robots and his sedan chair he ran down the marble steps. He had been worried about some of the machinery in the silver mine for the last few months and had been saving up for new equipment by playing his staff at poker, darts and shove-halfpenny for their wages. Now, the worst had happened.

Big Fat Joe tried to drag Bernard out of the house. The town had eventually been given the alarm by miners coming from the scene of the disaster.

"There's a flood. A miner is trapped in an air-bubble underground," Big Fat Joe said, "what a chance for you!"

"You go Dad, I think I'll stay at home and do my homework," Bernard sighed.

"I can't do anything! I'd get stuck in the shaft!" Big Fat Joe replied, prising Bernard's fingers off the door-jamb, bundling him into his orange drop-head Bugatti and driving like the wind towards El Dinero.

Bernard looked sideways at his father. He was moved by the knowledge that the ex-detective had smothered his own pride and ambition and was now building his dreams on his son—him, Bernard, a young buck with no experience. As the car shot through the gate and towards the winding-gear,

Bernard peered through the window to see if his rival was around. His heart sank when he caught sight of Horatio Upright donning a frogman's outfit and air-bottles. Big Fat Joe's sacrifice would be for nothing.

"I'll just find out what's cooking," Big Fat Joe murmured and slid his tubby form from behind the steering-wheel. "You stay here."

As Big Fat Joe reached the shaft-head, Horatio Upright was preparing to dive backwards into the flooded shaft. Sir George Mindbright Wilderness was wringing his wallet with grief. With a reassuring smile Horatio Upright launched himself into the water and disappeared in a stream of bubbles.

The crowd was silent, deeply impressed. All of them knew that Horatio Upright had done a fair bit of cheating lately with his heroics; hiring his cousin Nathan to dress up and threaten old ladies so they could be rescued at low risk; climbing trees to bring down stuffed cats which Horatio had put there the night before; setting fire to dustbins so he could put them out, but this was genuine. Horatio Upright was really doing his stuff.

Sir George Mindbright Wilderness looked at his watch. Horatio Upright had been down El Dinero for half an hour. Things were beginning to look black for the old hero. After an hour there was still no sign of him. The crowd sat down on the ground and became very sad, then they started looking at Sir George Mindbright Wilderness and muttering about how mean he was, how obsolete the pumps were down the mine.

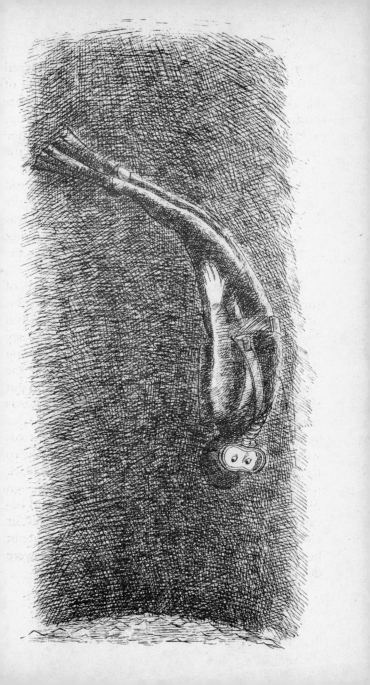

Cautiously Bernard got out of the car and sidled up to Sir George who was getting very agitated. The mine-owner could see the Bishop puffing up the slope towards the shaft on his bicycle with the kind of look on his face that threatened endless lectures and sermons. He could be denounced from the pulpit.

"Can't you do something Bernard old chap?" Sir George pleaded. "Don't let the Bishop get his teeth into me."

"Is there another entrance to the mine?" Bernard asked.

"No . . . hold on, yes, an old one which we don't use now. It's round the other side of the mountain," Sir George said, "but you can't use it. There's no ladderway or anything. It goes straight down. We only use it for ventilation."

"Perfect!" Bernard shouted. "Bang on! Dad, get in the shaft!"

"Get in?" Big Fat Joe protested. "I can't get in!"

"Yes you can, I bet you can just make it," Bernard insisted. "Hurry up. There's no time to lose."

Big Fat Joe got on top of the shaft and stuck his legs down, then squeezed himself into the collar. He couldn't manage it.

"Help me push him down," Bernard shouted to the crowd, "everyone give us a hand."

Slowly Big Fat Joe was pushed into the shaft like a cork into a bottle. He was so fat that the water couldn't get past his body. With everyone pushing him he started forcing the water back down the shaft. When the Bishop arrived and started delivering a stern remonstrance to Sir George, he was told to shut up by the crowd and to get his weight on top of Big Fat Joe. Soon the whole crowd was in the shaft on Big Fat Joe's head and shoulders and he was moving towards the bottom quite quickly.

"Right, let's go round to the old entrance," Bernard said to Sir George.

"I don't understand . . . ."

"Don't ask questions. Get your sedan chair moving," Bernard commanded. "There are two lives at stake."

When they arrived at the old entrance there were thousands of gallons of water pouring out. Bernard looked disappointed.

"They haven't arrived yet," he grieved.

"You're expecting them to come up here?" Sir George said wonderingly.

As he spoke a huge bubble of air slid up out of the shaft. Sitting in it were a man wearing a miner's helmet and clothes and a frogman with air-bottles on his back. The bubble left the water and floated off into the air towards Santa Margarita del Banana followed by Sir George and Bernard in the sedan chair carried by the robots, then by the crowd and the Bishop. They saw the bubble float over the side of the mountain. It crossed the woods and fields, the orchards and gardens, the roof-tops and the three red towers of the cathedral, then descended. It finally burst on the point of Ug the Indescribable's lightning-flash and the miner and Horatio Upright fell into the square.

Both men were safely home. Everyone agreed that Bernard's quick thinking had saved the day. It was only a few hours later when Horatio Upright was buying Bernard a Coke in Lugsy's cantina and explaining that there had been no real need for Bernard to come up with his idea because the old hero was only resting down there etc. etc., however, it was good practice for a beginner, that Bernard remembered his father. Where was Big Fat Joe?

Sir George lent Bernard his sedan chair and the robots trotted up to El Dinero at maximum speed. Bernard looked down the shaft and there was Big Fat Joe about halfway down.

"Ah," Bernard said, "you see what has happened Dad. Because the water has been displaced, the level in the shaft has fallen . . . ."

There was a silence from below. Big Fat Joe looked up at the circle of light with his son's head in it. He did not speak, but he did not need to. There was enough in his expression to make Bernard cut short his scientific explanation and arrange for a cable to be lowered and attached to his father's belt. When this had been done he signalled for the man at the winch to bring Big Fat Joe to the surface.

The ex-detective emerged from the shaft and hung in mid-air, water streaming from his enormous trousers.

"Bernard," he said.

"Yes, Dad?"

"Could you stay at your Auntie Millie's tonight?"

"Why, Dad?"

"Do you want to stay friends with your father?"

"Of course, Dad."

"Just keep away from me for twenty-four hours until I can appreciate what a child of genius you are," Big Fat Joe said bitterly as his feet touched the ground. "Get moving!"

Bernard ran all the way back to the town and left the sedan chair for his father. That night he stayed at his Auntie Millie's and waited for the newspaper to come out with the story of his latest exploit. As might be expected, the person who praised his deed most was his Physics master at school. He insisted on drawing a diagram for the class and tying the rescue in with a Greek person who shouted Eureka and ran naked down the street after jumping out of his bath, and also with the formula behind the hydraulic press whereby a small force at one place can produce a large force at another.

"In the past," the master said, "I have said unkind things about Bernard's Physics. But let it be said here and now, there is more rejoicing over one theory put into practice than all the text-books in the world."

CHAPTER SEVEN

Feeding the Birds

Santa Margarita del Banana was very short of birds. There were only a few varieties around and some of these were quite unpopular, such as the Vulture and the High-tailed Red Banana-bending Crow which was officially declared a pest by the Bishop from the pulpit a year ago, just before Christmas. These birds went out at night and deliberately bent all the bananas the other way and carried many of them back to their mountain roosts. The crops lost much of their value this way as what people wanted to buy overseas was the unusually curved fruit for which the town was famous, not ordinary, boring bananas.

Sir George Mindbright Wilderness had put the problem of the High-tailed Red Banana-bending Crow to a group of scientists and asked them for advice on how to deal with the flying menace. They suggested poison and shooting. These measures went against the grain and the town council voted them out, saying that they would rather suffer from warped bananas than guilty consciences.

The summer came and the banana crop suffered a

terrible plague of unlooked-for bending and theft. Desperate measures were called for. Horatio Upright built himself a crow-spraying aeroplane out of balsa wood and rice-paper but it crashed on take-off. Big Fat Joe put up the idea of bending all the bananas the wrong way first, then letting the crows bend them back the right way. This would have taken fifteen years and it was shelved, though the town council agreed that the idea proved that Big Fat Joe might be thick round the middle but he certainly was not thick in the head. Finally the Bishop himself came to see Bernard and encouraged him to outdo the adults yet again with a brilliant scheme.

"It would not be pride, or vanity, my son, but a public service. Flog your imagination and see what you can come up with. If we do not get rid of the High-tailed Red Banana-bending Crow before the harvest, we will be left with a crop of unsaleable fruit which we cannot shift. Wilt thou have a go?"

Bernard was flattered. He had plenty of homework to do that week but he agreed to try. That evening he went up one of the three red towers of the cathedral with the Bishop and together they watched the flocks of High-tailed Red Banana-bending Crows flying towards the plantations, cawing (or was it laughing?).

"A dreadful sight," the Bishop lamented. "What inspires the creatures to such wickedness? Wherefore do they persist in this senseless evil against the simple and symmetrical bananas? Yea verily, I am totally stumped."

From the plantations came the creaking of thousands of bananas being bent the wrong way. The Bishop covered up his ears and ran down the spiral stairs.

But Bernard stayed where he was, thinking.

It was a good question, and a good start to solving the problem. Why? Why? Why? What was in it for the High-tailed Red Banana-bending Crow to bend the bananas?

He stayed up in the tower for another hour until the moon rode up over the mountains and the crows flapped off into the darkness leaving tons of mauled fruit behind them.

As he often did when faced with the mysteries of Nature, Bernard went to see Senor Gonzalez Filth. He was not able to cast light on the reason behind the strange attacks of the crows on the bananas, but he suggested that Bernard accompany him on a trip into the mountains to talk to the Yuk Indians who live in the comfortable caves up there. This tribe knew a lot about the animal world and they respected Senor Gonzalez Filth as he had been a cave-dweller of sorts himself, and he had once done the chief a favour.

"We will go this weekend as I am not working overtime, there being no fiesta for a change. I will borrow a couple of mules. It will be just like the old days. I need a break anyway," Senor Gonzalez Filth said. "I'm quite looking forward to it."

On Saturday morning they set out on the mules and rode into the mountains. Senor Gonzalez Filth threw back his head and breathed the pure air, his dark eyes glittering with pleasure.

"I think I must have the blood of nomads in my veins," he said to Bernard who was already getting sore in the saddle as the mule jolted over the rocks, "and this is nothing but Nature's rubbish-dump. Look."

Huge boulders and steeples of rocks, deep river canyons, old volcanoes which had flickered out millions of years before, sand, gravel, all the rubbings and grindings of glaciers, the sediment of seas, the boilings-over of the hot centre of the earth, lay strewn all around.

"If I was a little bigger and had more time I might try and clear it up myself," joked Senor Gonzalez Filth as an arrow with a sucker on it slammed straight between his eyes and he fell off his mule into a cactus bush.

Bernard pulled hard on the reins as a boy his own age jumped from behind a rock. He had a red feather in his hair and was wearing nothing but a pair of trousers made of banana skins.

"What a way to treat an old friend of your people!" Senor Gonzalez Filth spluttered as he plucked cactus needles out of his backside. "I'll have something to say about this to Chief Almighty Pecker."

"I am the son of Chief Almighty Pecker and it is my job to guard the way to the caves. Who are you, O perforated and unwashed one?"

"Your father and I have hunted the buffalo to-gether . . . ."

"There are no buffalo up here, only the High-tailed Red Banana-bending Crow. What age are you living in, O reeking and irritated one?"

Not wanting to beg any more questions, Senor Gonzalez Filth stamped on the ground, threw the arrow away, danced a tantrum and a flamenco, waved his fists in the air and persuaded the youth to lead them into the presence of the chief.

"They only respect strength you know," Senor Gonzalez Filth whispered to Bernard. "Don't take

any nonsense from these Indians and they will treat you decently. Don't show any weakness."

When they arrived at the caves ten hours later they were very tired. Chief Almighty Pecker had seen them coming and had put aside a special cave for the travellers. When they had been given food and drink and had had a good lie-down, he paid them a visit.

He was a noble and dignified figure in his bonnet of red feathers. He offered Senor Gonzalez Filth a smoke of a peace-pipe which was shaped like a banana.

"It is good to see you my old and smouldering friend. I remember how you rescued me from the circus in Mexico City when I had been put into the dustbin for falling off my horse on the high-wire. If it had not been for you I would have found my way to the mechanical garbage-grinders and been shredded. Hau!"

"Hau!" Senor Gonzales Filth replied, covered in sweet-smelling smoke. "What is this tobacco?"

"Dried banana leaves, my odoriferous old buddy," Chief Almighty Pecker replied. "Nice isn't it?"

While the two old friends reminisced, Bernard's mind was moving very quickly. As the tribal dancing started and fifteen men and young girls swayed round and round dressed as bananas and High-tailed Red Banana-bending Crows, Bernard was beginning to unravel part of the problem. When he saw the dancers dressed as crows bending the bananas it all started falling into place.

"What does this dance mean Chief?" Bernard asked respectfully.

Chief Almighty Pecker thrust out his lower lip and his eyes took on a far-away look.

"It's a long story," he muttered, "and you wouldn't understand."

"Is it an old myth?"

"Myth? Look son, life is hard up here. We don't have time for myths. We're practical people. We get things done. Don't talk to me about myths."

At that moment a huge flock of High-tailed Red Banana-bending Crows flew cawing out of the highest caves in the settlement and streamed off in the direction of Santa Margarita del Banana.

"Do you know where those birds are going?" Bernard asked.

"Nothing to do with me," Chief Almighty Pecker grunted sourly. "I only do as I'm told by the medicine man, Little Aggressive Squirrel. Some people say *he* really rules the Yuk tribe. I'm not prepared to argue as it is not in my nature and besides, what does it matter?"

There was a silence as Senor Gonzalez Filth patted his old friend on the shoulder and pricked his fingers on some decorative porcupine quills.

"I think you'd better tell us all about it," he murmured grimly, "because if you don't there will be others who will come up here to sort this business out who will be less sympathetic. It is obvious that you are somehow responsible for the mess being made of Santa Margarita del Banana's plantations. If the Bishop gets up here . . . well, I pity you."

Chief Almighty Pecker started crying. He leant his face on his banana-skin trousers and wept and confessed that he was at his wit's end with the whole thing. Little Aggressive Squirrel and the High-tailed Red Banana-bending Crows had ruined his life.

"Best to share your grief old friend," Senor Gonzalez Filth said comfortingly. "Spit it out. We'll understand. Now, what's been going on?"

"The people of Santa Margarita del Banana have a great enemy in our medicine man, Little Aggressive Squirrel," Chief Almighty Pecker sighed. "He blames you for all our misfortunes. The land on which your town is built belongs to the Yuk tribe, so he says, and he is determined to drive you out."

"Do you agree with him at all?" Bernard asked the chief.

"No, son, I recognise the truth. We live up here in these caves because we like it. We pay no rent, rates or taxes and the slates never blow off the roof."

"Then why is he doing this?"

"Ambition, son, ambition. He wants to take over the tribe. A man who can train a whole flock of ordinary High-tailed Red Corn-cob-crumbling Crows to change their habits and start living off the natural oil given off by a bent banana is no slouch. He spent years up there with them. Little Aggressive Squirrel is so powerful that he has persuaded the whole Yuk tribe that they are unhappy when they are not."

An hour later the crows returned. As they flew over the caves a huge coloured blanket was held out by the Indians and the crows obediently dropped their stolen bananas into it and then flapped off to their roosts. Senor Gonzalez Filth and Bernard watched the Indians pile the bananas up. When it was as high as it would go without falling over, a figure dressed in a racoon fur, banana skins and red feathers, with Coca-Cola tins round its neck and a leather bucket over its head with eye-holes through which flashed mad, dangerous glances, mounted the pile of yellow fruit. In a high, squeaky voice it stirred the Indians up.

"Little Aggressive Squirrel?" Bernard said.

"Who else?" sniffed Chief Almighty Pecker. "The bane of my life."

"Why does he wear a leather bucket over his head?"

"He says that he has sworn an oath never to show his face until Santa Margarita del Banana has been brought to its knees," Chief Almighty Pecker replied.

Bernard was the kind of person who thinks things out, but he knew that if he was to stop the menace to his home town's future he must act swiftly. Getting to his feet he walked over and stood in front of the pile of bananas and the raging medicine man. With Senor Gonzalez Filth close behind him he raised a hand in the air.

"Who is this?" squeaked Little Aggressive Squirrel, his hands groping for two bananas which were stuck in his belt but were immediately recognised by Bernard as revolvers in heavy disguise. Reaching forward Bernard pulled the bottom bananas out of the pile and Little Aggressive Squirrel tumbled forward into the waiting arms of Senor Gonzalez Filth who held him tight while Bernard yanked the leather bucket off to reveal Diablo Dick, the desperado who had escaped from prison by building a vaulting-horse out of apple dumplings and somersaulting over the main gates while the guards were playing bingo.

"It only remains for me to speak to the crows," Bernard said as Diablo Dick was tied up and stuck on a mule with rattlesnake glue to stop him running away.

"Men cannot speak to crows, son," Chief Almighty Pecker pointed out. "They are just dumb birds."

"If this criminal can do it, I can do it!" Bernard insisted, and climbed up to the roosting caves. There he found a giant flock of very tired, oily and miserable crows. Diablo Dick had obviously trained them up from birth and the problem was how to get them off the banana as a main source of food. There was only one answer. Get back to Nature.

"I'll fix it," Bernard assured the chief. "Do you plant corn?"

"We have a few fields down in the valley there."

With the help of the Indians Bernard carried all the corn cobs they could find to the roosting caves and hung them up, covered with banana skins. The crows attacked the cobs, trying to bend them, but failed. As they struggled with the corn cobs, the kernels got into the birds' beaks down their throats and into their stomachs and they remembered what a pleasant thing a corn kernel is to eat. From that moment on they were converted back to their original food and only

stole from the corn fields of the Indians, which is what Nature had intended.

Diablo Dick was taken to Santa Margarita del Banana and tried in front of the magistrate, Sir George Mindbright Wilderness, for impersonating a medicine man. He was found guilty and sentenced to prison for ten years and a fortnight. The court recommended that apple dumplings and spaghetti be kept off the menu, but they made no mention of oxtail soup.

Bernard was given a hero's welcome, of course. By this time he was getting used to it and could shrug modestly which is a useful trick if you know how.

CHAPTER EIGHT

The Give-Away

Dormitory McBride's job came up for re-election. He was a popular sheriff and painstakingly fair. Not only would he snore through the crimes of the poor, but the rich as well. If Senor Gonzalez Filth had decided to go mad and set fire to the cathedral, Dormitory McBride would have taken the same refuge as he would if the arson had been committed by Sir George Mindbright Wilderness—in the arms of Morpheus, the god of sleep. Also he had another advantage. Those people who broke the law in order to draw attention to themselves got no encouragement from Dormitory. He ignored them and stayed with his dreams, boots up on his hitching-rail.

Truth to tell, Dormitory was well covered by the activities of Bernard and, to a lesser extent, Horatio Upright. They combated what crime there was in Santa Margarita del Banana and if there was any left over after they had finished being brave and ingenious, Big Fat Joe did some part-time work on it in his retirement.

So this system trundled along quite efficiently until

the time came when these three crimefighters were defeated by an outbreak of boot-lace stealing and, unfortunately for Dormitory, this happened in the month before the re-election. In the town council there were harsh words said about a sheriff who spent all his time snoozing and it had to be admitted that these criticisms were deserved.

"You'll have to sharpen up a bit, Dormitory," Big Fat Joe told the sheriff over a drink in Lugsy's cantina, "otherwise you'll end up losing your job."

"I try, I do. Shucks I've been running around on the trail of that boot-lace stealing crittur for two weeks. I've been in the saddle for so long I'm saddle-sore . . . ."

"But you shouldn't ride around fast asleep in that contraption the blacksmith made up for you," Big Fat Joe insisted. "It doesn't look too good when the town

council see what trouble you take to relax on the job."

Dormitory McBride had saved up his wages and designed a special sleeping-frame for his horse. When it was fitted and strapped on, there was a pillow for his head, rests for his arms and a clock-radio which made tea between his horse's ears (the alarm on the clock had rusted because it had never been used). The stirrups on Dormitory's horse were not in the usual place but carried round the animal's back end so he could lie full-length. If you work this out you will see that he rode back-to-front and used a driving-mirror to see where he was going.

The whole job had cost him twenty-seven pesos and fourteen pence.

"Why shouldn't I be comfortable? Mine's a thinking job, Big Fat Joe, I don't have to be tensed up all the time. You know that yourself. Don't rush into things, is my motto . . . zzzzzzzzzz"

Dormitory fell asleep after the effort of this long speech, his nose slowly descending into the glass of sarsaparilla. All the customers watched with interest as the bubbles from the black fizzy drink went up the sheriff's nose and woke him up.

Their good-natured comments on the scene were interrupted by Sergeant Leonard Flytrifle stamping into the cantina with his boots rattling around his ankles.

"You useless son of a prairie schooner!" the old soldier yelled. "Look at this! While I was wearing them! Wearing them! Not only that, but I was marching, man, marching along with a bit of a swing. I get my boot-laces stolen in transit, mate, actually on the move! And what are you doing? Having a kip again. It's not good enough, you horrible streak of stagnant pond-water! I'd fire you tomorrow!"

"Sorry Sergeant," Dormitory mumbled in between sneezes as the sarsaparilla tickled the back of his throat, "I'll dust your boots for finger-prints."

"Finger-prints! Whatever is stealing these laces hasn't got fingers, you hopeless heap of old eyewash and humbug! It must be magic! I was actually doing a fair pace, arms going up in the approved style when, Whissssh! They'd gone. Didn't feel a thing. Sort it out, shun! Left right left right left right!"

Sergeant Leonard Flytrifle dragged Dormitory McBride to his feet and frogmarched him down to his sheriff's office and made a full report, demanding that a wanted poster be issued. It was printed and circulated the next morning.

This poster did no good at all. Dormitory McBride became a laughing-stock. It was plain that Sergeant Leonard Flytrifle had dictated it and the sheriff had just given in to his imperious demands.

"The question is, can we really afford to have a sheriff who doesn't know what he's doing and can be so easily pushed around?" Sir George Mindbright Wilderness said in confidence to the Bishop over dinner that night as they discussed the forthcoming election and whom they should support. "Up till now he's had an easy time because we have Bernard,

REWARD 10 PESOS 7½ PENCE

?

WANTED

Invisible, magical, low-down,
thieving robber who strikes
army pensioners on the trot.
Has a taste for boot-laces
which have seen action. If
cornered approach only in
bare feet.

Big Fat Joe and old Horatio . . . but the true situation
has been exposed by this outbreak of boot-lace thefts.
We haven't got a sheriff at all, we've got a present
incumbent who's always recumbent."

While all this was going on, Bernard was hard at
work on the problem of the recent crime-wave. He
had seen the suffering caused by the lack of boot-laces
in the town (the shops had been hit by panic-buying
very early on) and how people were continually
falling over or stepping on to the bus and leaving their
boots behind because there was nothing to hold them

on to their feet. Three citizens were already in hospital with toe-cramp through walking around trying to keep their footwear on by curling their toes up tight and walking in a strange, stiff way. If the outrages carried on at their present rate it would not be long before the entire population of Santa Margarita del Banana was flat on its back.

When the rumours started to spread that Dormitory McBride was going to be given the order of the boot from his job as sheriff, Bernard worked even harder. He was very fond of the sleeping law officer, both as an individual and because having such a lazy sheriff meant there were more opportunities for detection and heroics.

"It can't be human," he reasoned, "but it could be something familiar like a bird. It could be a bird that thinks the boot-laces are worms. Yes, that could be it . . . ."

He watched the skies with Big Fat Joe's binoculars. All he saw were Vultures and High-tailed Red Corncorn-cob-crumbling Crows. While he had the binoculars trained on Little Jim Winze who was crossing the square he suddenly saw the boy's boot-laces whipped out as if by an unseen hand and the poor lad fall over.

Bernard gasped in amazement.

"It's magic!" he breathed. "My first magical criminal! This is marvellous."

Running out into the square, Bernard picked his friend up and asked him questions about the theft. Had he seen anything? Heard anything?

"I was just walking along and suddenly my boots started falling off. I didn't feel a thing till then . . . ." Little Jim Winze spluttered, spitting out the yellow dust which lay over everything that summer. "I wouldn't have believed it possible if it hadn't happened to me, personally."

"I'm really up against a cunning foe this time. Right under my nose . . . ."

"No, my nose!" said Little Jim Winze ruefully rubbing his which he had banged when he fell over.

The thefts went on and on until the day before the elections for the post of sheriff. Dormitory McBride was standing again but he knew that he had no support. The official candidate who had the backing of the town council was Hairy von Rjin who still had a reputation as a tough guy because of the way he had

helped to capture Diablo Dick. Hairy had agreed to
stand for election but insisted that he would have to
run the job with that of town barber.

"What happens if I can't catch the boot-lace burg-
lar? You'll throw me out of office and I won't have a
job," he explained to the town council. "It's obvious
that we're up against a master criminal. I'll have a go,
but if I fail I want something to fall back on."

What could they say? Hairy von Rjin's idea made
double sense. It occurred to Sir George Mindbright
Wilderness that to have a town without boot-laces
was dangerous enough, but to have a town where
everyone had very long hair because there was no
barber was making the situation much worse.

"We would never get back on our feet. We would
always be tripping up, falling down. It would en-
courage catastrophe," he said to the town council as
he seconded Hairy's proposal of running his two
jobs.

That evening there was a cloudburst. The rain
poured out of the sky. Streams from the mountains
became torrents and flooded the streets and the
square. Within an hour it was all over and the water
had drained into the sea, leaving the town wet and
shining.

Bernard was the first to come out after the storm
had abated. Playing a hunch he walked round and
round the square in a pair of boots with very long
laces which flapped about. It was starting to get dark
and everyone else in Santa Margarita del Banana was
wringing out their sitting-room linoleum.

Suddenly a yellow flash shot across from the rubbish-dump where Senor Gonzalez Filth was drying out the garbage with a hair-dryer and cursing the rain in colourful Spanish. The yellow flash struck Bernard's boots like a fork of lightning and tore out his laces, then turned and shot off, but not before Bernard had taken a photograph of it with his camera and flash-gun.

Hurrying home he rushed into Big Fat Joe's study, asked if he could use the ex-detective's dark room and within an hour he had developed and printed the photograph that should have gone on the Wanted poster.

"What is it?" Bertha Boom-Boom asked from under her latest hair-do which was based on a melted typewriter she had seen in a burnt-out newspaper office in New Jersey during her summer holidays. "What a funny thing!"

"It's a mongoose," Bernard explained, "an Indian mongoose."

"What is it doing here?" Big Fat Joe demanded, sucking on his cherrywood pipe which was carved in the shape of a Christmas cake.

"I don't know, but I think it's a young one. They eat snakes and this mongoose has got mixed up between snakes and boot-laces. See how thin it is."

"Why didn't we see it before?"

"The summer dust. It's exactly the same colour as its fur. It's camouflaged in the dust. And that reminds me of a place I might find it hiding out."

"Where?"

"The rubbish-dump. The mongoose has obviously been watching Senor Gonzalez Filth at work. He understands camouflage like no one else. When he's in there with all the rubbish you can't see him at all, and I remember his first lesson when he stole the workman's lunch . . . ."

Then Bernard paused and thought a while. He thought about how Dormitory McBride must be feeling. In the last couple of years Bernard had enjoyed many triumphs and the sheriff had never begrudged him his success.

"Dad, you and Bertha are the only people who know about this. I want you to swear that you will never tell anyone else . . . ."

"But Bernard, you've made a brilliant case of this. You have a photograph of the criminal actually in the act. No one else would have thought of it. You deserve a pat on the back and the reward," Big Fat Joe said warmly. "Go on, take what is yours."

Bernard shook his head and made Big Fat Joe and Bertha Boom-Boom swear to keep his master-stroke a secret, then went along to Dormitory McBride's office and told him the story.

"Wish I could be smart, like you," Dormitory McBride said wistfully as he looked at the photograph, "but I ain't and I'm going to be out on my ear come sundown tomorrow, sure as anything."

"Not if you do as I say," Bernard smiled. "All we'll need is a pair of boot-laces."

"Boot-laces? But that's one thing you can't get hold of since this little crittur got to sidewinding everybody's feet," Dormitory replied in dismay. "There isn't a pair left in town."

"Oh yes there is, look!" Bernard pulled a pair of boot-laces out of his pocket and waved them in the air. "They're out of my Dad's old rugger boots which I found in the attic. These will be our bait."

The voting for the election opened at ten o'clock the following morning and long queues formed outside the booth which had been put up next to the statue to Ug the Indescribable. Just as the door of the booth opened to admit the first voter, Dormitory McBride walked across the square in a huge pair of boots.

"Look at that! Wouldn't you think he'd be ashamed! The only pair of boot-laces in town and he's wearing them . . . ."

"Flaunting them at us, that's what he's doing, the dopey old deadbeat!"

Hisses, boos and jeers rose from the queue. Dormitory McBride marched on. Bernard watched from the belfry of one of the cathedral towers, his fingers crossed.

He saw the Indian mongoose streak out of the rubbish-dump and across the square. It sprang at the flapping boot-laces and pulled. Sparks flew and the mongoose stiffened. Dormitory McBride took a large canvas bag out of his waistcoat pocket and bundled the mongoose into it, first turning off a switch hidden under the brim of his ten litre hat.

"There's your boot-lace bandit!" he shouted. "And I fooled him a treat. I've got two powerful batteries in

the heels of my huge boots and wires down the length
of the laces. This mongoose has been pole-axed by
electric shock, but he'll be all right later on. I worked
it out all by myself. We couldn't see him before
because he was the same colour as the dust, yes
sir—r—r—r—r—rrrrrrrrrrr."

Exhausted with this long speech, Dormitory fell
asleep with the mongoose clutched to his chest. The
crowd that had gathered round him were tremend-
ously impressed and streamed through the booth,
giving Dormitory their votes. Hairy von Rjin was
glad to admit defeat and voted for Dormitory himself. What people could not understand was how the
sheriff had managed to work out such a brilliant trap
for the thief, but they took it on trust. They thought
his brain had come to life because his livelihood was
threatened. When they saw him fast asleep in his
rocking-chair with his boots on the hitching-rail
again the next day they all thought he was thinking.

The Indian mongoose was sent back home to India.
No one knew how it had got to Santa Margarita del
Banana, but I can tell you. It had walked from India
to Tibet, from Tibet to China, from China to Manchuria, from Manchuria to Siberia, from Siberia to
the Bering Straits which it had swum and landed on the
other side in Alaska, then down the Rocky Mountains
through Canada, the United States of America,
Mexico . . . turned left at a mountain called Popo-
catepti . . . and arrived at Santa Margarita del Banana
after a week's journey through deserts and mountains.

No wonder it was hungry.

CHAPTER NINE

Furniture Removals Made Simple

As Sir George Mindbright Wilderness walked into the square he was met by his butler who was shaking like a leaf, white as a sheet and sick as a dog.

"What is it man? Speak up. Don't hold anything back. I can take it. I'm ready. Spit it out. Don't be afraid . . ." said Sir George kindly. "Let me have it, straight between the eyes. What's new?"

"Someone has stolen The Bumble Bee's Nest, your worship," the butler stammered.

"My house?" Sir George thundered. "Stolen my house? How?"

"I went into the kitchen garden to pull some radishes. As I was bending over and obtaining these small red root vegetables which are nice in salads, I heard a noise. Turning, I observed The Bumble Bee's Nest disappearing over the horizon. It has my wages in it."

Sir George Mindbright Wilderness sat down on the ground and held his head in his hands. He loved his old palatial mansion. He loved its marble pillars, its chandeliers and its billiard-table.

"Did they take any of the out-buildings?" he whispered tragically.

"No, your worship, only the stables and the palm-house and I haven't checked but I think they might have taken the rose-garden."

"My beautiful rose-garden where I love to sit in the evening and read Shakespeare and play the cello . . . my stables . . . did they take the horses?"

The butler nodded dumbly, then huskily croaked out a reminder.

"And, at the risk of repeating myself, your worship, my wages."

"Ask Bernard, Big Fat Joe, Horatio Upright and Dormitory McBride to meet me in Lugsy's cantina in ten minutes," Sir George commanded with sudden fierceness. "This calls for an all-out effort."

The four heroes and detectives of Santa Margarita del Banana stared at the empty space that had once held The Bumble Bee's Nest and out-buildings. It was true. It had gone.

"There may be a trail we can follow," Big Fat Joe said thoughtfully. "Let's have a look round."

Sure enough, they found tracks nearby.

"Feet," Horatio Upright murmured as he identified the marks in the earth, "lots of feet, about fifty pairs of feet."

"Heading west," Dormitory McBride noticed. Then, being reminded of evening and night by the fact that the sun sets in the west, he nodded off and fell into a clump of tumbleweed which was passing. The tumbleweed tumbled the sheriff along behind

Big Fat Joe's orange drop-head Bugatti as it was driven along the trail left by the palace-pilferers.

After three hours' driving through the desert they came to a river. Floating downstream on eighty-six forty-four gallon oil drums was The Bumble Bee's Nest. It was being poled along by men leaning out of the windows singing:

> "They put me in the chain-gang
> For doin' wrong,
> With the help of my friend Deedee
> Ah didn't stay long.
> Goin' to pole this palace
> Way down to the sea,
> Where ah'll sell it to someone
> For plenty money.
>
> Oxtail soup foh dinner, oxtail soup foh tea,
> Oxtail soup has kinda made me feel fancy-free.
> Yeh, Deedee is the man for me,
> Deedee is the man for me, yeh, yeh,
> Come storm or hot weather
> Ah'll work hell for leather
> For old Deedee, yeh, yeh."

As the orange drop-head Bugatti drove after The Bumble Bee's Nest the men poled faster and shots were fired, kicking up the sand around the car. Big Fat Joe stopped and put the hand-brake on.

"They're obviously professionals," he said grimly. "We'll have to think this one out to the last detail."

Having made their plan they followed The Bumble

Bee's Nest at a safe distance until nightfall and then drove along the bank without headlamps on, following the house which was blazing with electric light from every window as the thieves had attached the butler's bicycle to the generator and were taking it in turns to pedal it. Meanwhile, in the master bedroom, their leader was putting a message in a container round the leg of a High-tailed Red Banana-bending Crow (the last one in the world to stay loyal).

"Take this to the estate agent in Saint Louis, and bring back what price he's prepared to offer," the leader said. "This old pile should fetch a good price in the United States. We can have it there by spring."

The crow flew out of the window. There was a knock at the door of the master bedroom and a voice called:

"Deedee, can we stop polin' for the night and make camp. The boys are sure beat from all that carryin' over the desert and now all this sailin'. How's about it Deedee?"

"Keep it movin'," Deedee replied curtly. "We're bein' followed."

It would be unfair to keep anyone in suspense a moment longer. The leader of the thieves, Deedee, was none other than Diablo Dick. He had escaped from prison by saving up all the oxtail soup served to him in his cell until he only had enough space to stick his nose out and breathe. Then he had called for the warder. The warder had opened the cell door and been bowled over by a tidal wave of oxtail soup which had swept down the corridor, out of the door, and poured over the wall carrying Diablo Dick and all the other men in his block with it.

Then Diablo Dick had formed a gang to steal Sir George Mindbright Wilderness's house and get his revenge for being sentenced to twenty years and a fortnight in the slammer.

How much he'll get for *this* crime is anybody's guess.

The next morning saw The Bumble Bee's Nest approaching an island in the river. Diablo Dick was pleased to see trees growing on it and ordered the gang to pole the house up to the island so they could cut some wood for the fires as the nights were cold and the electric fires used up too much electricity and exhausted the men who pedalled the bicycle.

As Diablo Dick stepped on to the island he hesitated.

"Ground's sure soft around here," he said.

As soon as he was safely on the island it started moving. Bernard and Horatio Upright jumped out of the trees and took away Diablo Dick's revolver.

"All right Dad, keep backstroking," Bernard called to Big Fat Joe who was the island and had branches stuck in his pants.

Once the gang knew that their leader had been arrested by this ruse of pure genius, they gave up, confessing that they could not imagine having much of a chance against such crimefighting talent. Under the watchful eye of Big Fat Joe (who caught a cold, sad to say), Horatio Upright and Bernard (Dormitory

tumbled along the bank still, oblivious to all this), the gang of convicts poled The Bumble Bee's Nest down to the river mouth, then up the coast back to Santa Margarita del Banana.

When Sir George Mindbright Wilderness saw his house sailing into the harbour he broke down and wept with happiness. When the butler looked for his wages in his room he cracked up and wept with vexation. Diablo Dick had already spent the money on hamburgers from a travelling salesman.

Diablo Dick was sentenced to forty years and a month by Sir George but this had to be reduced to nothing when his lawyer pointed out that there was breaking and entering, there was robbery and theft, but no law had ever been passed forbidding stealing a house, only its contents; so Sir George did him for

stealing the butler's wages which were six pesos three pence. For this Diablo Dick got sixty years and six weeks because of his record. Spaghetti, apple dumplings and oxtail soup were not to be included on the menu while he was in prison but no mention was made of stuffed green peppers.

The four heroes and detectives never let on who it was that had thought up the scheme which had trapped Diablo Dick and recovered The Bumble Bee's Nest.

It seems a bit beyond Dormitory McBride. I can't imagine Big Fat Joe suggesting that he should get another ducking. Horatio Upright might have come up with it in a million years.

Seems a foregone conclusion, so good-bye.

Heard about the Puffin Club?

... it's a way of finding out more about Puffin books and authors, of winning prizes (in competitions), sharing jokes, a secret code, and perhaps seeing your name in print! When you join you get a copy of our magazine, *Puffin Post*, sent to you four times a year, a badge and a membership book.

For details of subscription and an application form, send a stamped addressed envelope to:

The Puffin Club Dept A
Penguin Books Limited
Bath Road
Harmondsworth
Middlesex UB7 0DA

and if you live in Australia, please write to:

The Australian Puffin Club
Penguin Books Australia Limited
P.O. Box 257
Ringwood
Victoria 3134